Copyright © 2018 Be 4 Real Publishing

All rights reserved.

ISBN: **978-1720335610**

ISBN-13: **1720335613**

are so happy he's divorcing. I mean you had your chance with him and you allowed him to go away and did not bother to change your mind. "Fentress picked up her ice water as three set of eyes leveled on her. "What?"

"Guess it's a good thing no one asked you what you thought then. I think December is telling us that he is divorcing his wife because she obviously knows she made a mistake. She does not need your turned-up nose reminding her that she let him go." Chaniyah was ready to blow a fuse. Of the four friends, her and Fentress bumped heads most often. They disagreed about almost everything.

"Well, I'm just saying-"

"Nobody asked you to just say anything." Chaniyah cut in.

"Okay ladies, put the claws back." December interjected. "We only get together occasionally and I don't want to spend it with the two of you arguing. I just thought you know since he was divorcing, maybe I can finally tell him what a mistake I made and you know, see if I can try and make things better. You know, for Destiny's sake."

"Girl you aren't fooling anyone, you know you trying to make things better for them cob webs you have forming between your legs." Chaniyah said laughing and slapping fives with Amari.

"Sorry D.K., but that was kind of funny." Amari said when December glared at her. When Fentress just shook her head, and sipped her water, Chaniyah leaned over and whispered to Amari, "Speaking of which, Queen Fefe, so needs to get laid. Maybe then she'll get her head and nose out of the clouds."

Amari nearly choked on her drink and Fentress cut her eyes at Chaniyah.

"You know what?" Fentress exclaimed, "I have to be to work. I don't have time for this foolishness."

"All Fefe, I thought you were going to get off, we hardly ever chill anymore." December pouted.

"I know D.K. but duty calls. Besides," she said staring straight at Chaniyah. "The sooner I get the money up, the sooner I can get my own place like you did."

"Oh, don't be like that Fentress, you know I'm just playing with you. You could never take a joke." Chaniyah chimed in.

"You know I hate that name."

"Oh, my bad, queen Fefe," Chaniyah said with just a hint of sarcasm.

"See," she said leaning in to hug December, "I will talk to you later girl. Kiss Destiny for me. I will see you other two later."

"See you girl," they all exclaimed in unison.

"Chaniyah, why are you always so hard on Fentress, you know she catches feelings fast." December asked once Fentress was out of earshot.

"It's been three years since Davon broke her heart, does she have to be so miserable I mean gosh, she always killing the vibe. I be tempted to ask my dude does he have a friend that will jump her bones so she can loosen up a little bit. Next thing you know, she gone become a nun."

"See, this is why we can't take you anywhere, girl you are crazy," Amari said before they all started laughing.

"She will come around eventually. You know she really loved Davon and he led her on all that time and then dropped a bombshell when he told her he was married. She was devastated. That is why she has such strong emotions about this situation." December always tried to see reason between the four friends. She was the calm and peaceful one.

"Well what is your plan?" Amari asked.

"I haven't really thought about it. I mean I am happy that he is getting divorced but that does not exactly mean that he is still interested in being with me." They all nodded in agreement.

"I just want to give Destiny the opportunity to

have what I didn't have growing up; a two-parent household. I wish I would have stuck by him back then."

"D.K. you cannot beat yourself up about something that happened over seven years ago. All you can do is plead your case now and hope that there is a chance for you and if not, well you and Marcel owe it to Destiny to be the best parents that you all can be to her." Both December and Chaniyah agreed.

The rest of the lunch date the longtime friends caught up on the day to day happenings of one another. December and Amari had been childhood friends who had eventually went to college together but shared two different interest in studies. Where December studied physical therapy, Amari had studied business management. They had met Chaniyah and Fentress in college when the four had shared a dorm. Now almost ten years later and they were still very close friends.

Although each had very different career paths, they all had one thing in common, they were loyal to a fault and successful each in their own way. December was now a physical therapist at Rehab You, a local rehabilitation facility that was ranked number one in the region. Amari owned an accounting firm serving some of the state's leading men and women. She was proud of her business and had recently been featured in Essence as one of the leading ladies.

Fentress was head nurse for the local ER. It was not uncommon for her to work 48 hours at a time. She often came home showered and then was right back out the door to work. She didn't work that way "Marcel is getting a divorce," December was beaming as she revealed the latest news pertaining to the father of her now seven-year-old daughter Destiny. They had spent three years together and when December revealed that she was pregnant, she thought that Marcel would give her a marriage proposal. Instead, he had told her that he wanted to join the military and try and make a life for her and their unborn child. Unhappy with his decision she had broken up with him. When he returned married, he crushed her heart and her dream of making the situation right.

"Okay I have never heard someone so happy for some other woman's demise," Fentress said as the more level-headed woman in the group. "I mean, there are two people affected by this decision and whether he is happy about it or not, still remains a topic."

"Uh, do you always have to be so philosophical," Chaniyah chimed in. "It's obvious he has come to his senses and realized that December is the only person for him and he is coming to sweep her off her feet." She takes a sip of her margarita. "Besides, I never liked his ex-wife anyway. If she was to ever put a hand on Destiny, I will lay my hands on her. "

"Chaniyah, you are so violent all of the time," Amari, the last of the clan added. "Besides, when did you become the helpless romantic, last I checked, you still won't stay past two minutes after having sex with a guy. You were a man in your previously life."

Everyone started to laugh. "Amari, why you telling my business? Besides, you all should be taking notes, you won't catch me stalking a guy's mom trying to get the latest information on his whereabouts and his coming and going. I like my way of thinking; Get what you want and get out of there before that man has a chance to expect more than he's going to get. "

"December, ignore her." Amari said recapturing the attention of her best friend. "Chaniyah you sound like a male. I look forward to the day when some guy can come in and rock your world and when you fall, you are going to fall hard. Mark my words."

"I am not going out like that." Chaniyah exclaimed.

"Anyway, personally I think it's horrible that you are so happy he's divorcing. I mean you had your chance with him and you allowed him to go away and did not bother to change your mind. "Fentress picked up her ice water as three set of eyes leveled on her. "What?"

"Guess it's a good thing no one asked you what

you thought then. I think December is telling us that he is divorcing his wife because she obviously knows she made a mistake. She does not need your turned-up nose reminding her that she let him go." Chaniyah was ready to blow a fuse. Of the four friends, her and Fentress bumped heads most often. They disagreed about almost everything.

"Well, I'm just saying-"

"Nobody asked you to just say anything." Chaniyah cut in.

"Okay ladies, put the claws back." December interjected. "We only get together once in a while and I don't want to spend it with the two of you arguing. I just thought you know since he was divorcing, maybe I can finally tell him what a mistake I made and you know, see if I can try and make things better. You know, for Destiny's sake."

"Girl you aren't fooling anyone, you know you trying to make things better for them cob webs you have forming between your legs." Chaniyah said laughing and slapping fives with Amari.

"Sorry D.K., but that was kind of funny." Amari said when December glared at her. When Fentress just shook her head and sipped her water, Chaniyah leaned over and whispered to Amari, "Speaking of which, Queen FeFe, so needs to get laid. Maybe then she'll get her head and nose out of the clouds."

Amari nearly choked on her drink and Fentress cut her eyes at Chaniyah.

"You know what?" Fentress exclaimed, "I have to be to work. I don't have time for this foolishness."

"All FeFe, I thought you were going to get off, we hardly ever chill anymore." December pouted.

"I know D.K. but duty calls. Besides," she said staring straight at Chaniyah. "The sooner I get the money up, the sooner I can get my own place like you did."

"Oh, don't be like that Fentress, you know I'm just playing with you. You could never take a joke." Chaniyah chimed in.

"You know I hate that name."

"Oh, my bad, queen FeFe," Chaniyah said with just a hint of sarcasm.

"See," she said leaning in to hug December, "I will talk to you later girl. Kiss Destiny for me. I will see you other two later."

"See you girl," they all exclaimed in unison.

"Chaniyah, why are you always so hard on Fentress, you know she catches feelings fast." December asked once Fentress was out of earshot.

"It's been three years since Davon broke her heart, does she have to be so miserable I mean gosh, she always killing the vibe. I be tempted to ask my dude does he have a friend that will jump her bones so she can loosen up a little bit. Next thing you know, she gone become a nun."

"See, this is why we can't take you anywhere, girl you are crazy," Amari said before they all started laughing.

"She will come around eventually. You know she really loved Davon and he led her on all that time and then dropped a bombshell when he told her he was married. She was devastated. That is why she has such strong emotions about this situation." December always tried to see reason between the four friends. She was the calm and peaceful one.

"Well what is your plan?" Amari asked.

"I haven't really thought about it. I mean I am happy that he is getting divorced but that does not exactly mean that he is still interested in being with me." They all nodded in agreement.

"I just want to give Destiny the opportunity to have what I didn't have growing up; a two-parent household. I wish I would have stuck by him back then."

"D.K. you cannot beat yourself up about something that happened over seven years ago. All you can do is plead your case now and hope that there is a chance for you and if not, well you and Marcel owe it to Destiny to be the best parents that you all can be to her." Both December and Chaniyah agreed.

The rest of the lunch date the longtime friends caught up on the day to day happenings of one another. December and Amari had been childhood friends who had eventually went to college together but shared two different interest in studies. Where December studied physical therapy, Amari had studied business management. They had met Chaniyah and Fentress in college when the four had shared a dorm. Now almost ten years later and they were still very close friends. because she needed the money, because she made very good money. She had been working that way since Davon dropped the bomb on her three years ago. Still to this day, it was an untouchable topic.

Chaniyah had become a couple therapist and had her own practice in town called Fix It Up. She has been credited by many of her patients with helping to restore their marriages back to their former glory and in some cases, making them better. No one understood how she could encourage people to stay together for a living and live the lifestyle she does.

After leaving her friends, December climbed into her Escalade and drove to Rehab You, where they were expecting her and put in a few hours of work before picking Destiny up from Marcel's mother at 8:00 PM. She loved that his mom was there to help out with Destiny and she appreciated being able to leave Destiny with family and not strangers. On the ride to Marcel's mother's house she started thinking about her life and how it could have been. *No use beating myself down now, she thought. But what is my plan.* She stopped at a red light and put her head on the steering wheel. Whatever her plan was going to be it had better be a good one. A car horn blared behind her snapping her out of her trance. She waved her hand and continued on until she arrived to Ms. Hamil's house. When she got there, she was greeted at the door by Destiny.

"Hi mommy, I missed you." She exclaimed.

She wrapped Destiny in a tight embrace. "Mommy missed you too baby. Did you have fun with grandma?" she asked carrying the oversized child into the living room of Ms. Hamil's home. "Hello Ms. Hamil. I hope Destiny wasn't a bother."

"Chile please, "she waved her off. "I always enjoy my grandchild's company. We baked cookies and walked to the park. She reminds me so much of Marcel when he was a kid, just a girl version." December smiled down at Destiny. She did look just like Marcel. The only thing she had taken from her was her light complexion. Although both her and Marcel were light skinned.

"You know Marcel will be in town in two weeks." Ms. Hamil said breaking into December's intimate moment with her child.

"Is that right?" she asked trying to take the enthusiasm out of her voice. "I'm sure Destiny can't wait to see her father, right Destiny?" She said, staring down at the young girl. She shook her head.

"Destiny, what did grandma tell you about shaking your head. Dummies shake their heads and you my child are no dummy." Destiny smiled over at her grandma.

"I can't wait to see daddy." December checked her watch and then sent Destiny to get her bag. "Come on sweetheart, mommy has an early day tomorrow and I still need to get you bathed for bed."

Destiny ran into the room to retrieve her bag.

"You know dear, I'm sure Marcel will be glad to see Destiny, but I am sure he will also be glad to see you as well." December blushed three shades of crimson.

"Why on earth would he want to see me?"

"Chile, are you that naïve? That boy was in love with you. He thought the world of you and when you broke up with him, you tore his world up. I am almost convinced he married that girl to try and get over you."

"But it's been over seven years, surely he cannot be still pining over me." She said for the sake of saying it, although she was hoping like hell that the latter was true. Before Ms. Hamil could respond, Destiny reentered the room.

"I'm ready mommy." She exclaimed.

"Okay baby, give grandma a kiss and hug."

Destiny raced over to her grandma and she was embraced in a deep hug and given a peck on the cheek. "I will see you in the morning my dear." Ms. Hamil said before releasing the child.

After December had gotten Destiny settled in for the evening, she showered and got ready for bed. As she lay there she kept thinking about what Ms. Hamil had said. What if Marcel was in fact still in love with her? What was she going to do about it? How would they get back to what they had? Was it even possible that they could get back there? Would he harbor resentment? Should he? At the rate she was going, she wouldn't be getting much sleep. She glanced over at the digital clock on the nightstand. It was 10:15. She wondered if Amari was up. It was times like these that she missed living with her friends. She'd probably still be living there now if she didn't have Destiny. She just wanted to raise her daughter in the private confines of

December. She works the night shift tomorrow. Maybe from the airport, we could go have lunch."

"Sounds like a plan mama, is Destiny there now, I would like to speak to my princess."

"Hold on, let me get her," Ms. Hamil said calling out to the young girl. Moment later, her voice bounced on the line.

"Daddy?" she exclaimed.

"It's me princess. How's daddy's big girl today?"

"I'm good daddy, grandma said you will be here tomorrow, is that true?"

Marcel smiled. It had been a whole two years since he'd seen his baby girl and it was two years too many. He hoped that he could convince December that her and Destiny could join him and be a family. He didn't like being away from his only child.

"Yes, baby, daddy's flight lands around three o'clock tomorrow afternoon."

"I can't wait to see you daddy, I made a book with all of the stuff I have been doing the past two years. It was mom's idea. She said that I could keep everything for when you came back so it would be like you never left."

"Well I can't wait to see it sweetheart. I love

you."

"I love you too daddy."

"Tell grandma I will call her when my plane gets close tomorrow okay."

"Okay daddy, bye." She said hanging up the phone.

It was just like December to think of him. That is what he loved about her. She didn't have a selfish bone in her body. Unlike the witch that he called wife for seven years. He was so glad that he was closing that chapter in his life and he looked forward to opening a new chapter that included December and Destiny, full time. Hopefully.

...

"Grandma, there's daddy!" Marcel turned to see his daughter running full speed towards him. He had to fight back the tears at seeing his baby girl. She was growing up so fast and he felt guilty for being absent from her life for the past two years. She jumped into his arms and he held on, afraid to let go. His mom just stood back and gave him this intimate moment with his child. He kissed the top of her head.

"Gosh, I've missed you baby girl." He said still

holding her tight. "Hey mama, how are you?" He said glancing over at his mother.

"Better now that my son is home," was her simple response.

"Shall we do lunch, daddy is starving?" he said pulling back to take a long glance at Destiny. "You are beautiful, just like your mother, you know that?"

"But mommy says that I look just like you daddy."

Marcel took a long hard glance at his daughter. "Does she now?" Destiny started to shake her head but then looked over to her grandma and thought better of it.

"Yes sir, she does." He simply smiled and kissed her again on the cheek. "So, about that lunch? Will you two lovely ladies lead the way, I'm starving."

Destiny dominated the majority of lunch, telling Marcel about first grade and how she had made honor roll all four marking periods. She would stop long enough to bite a nugget before she would proceed. Just as well, Marcel thought. It had been two whole years. *My little girl is going to be a second grader soon, he thought. Time sure does not stand still. I hope she doesn't think that I am deserting her.*

"And daddy, this year mommy says that the work is going to get a little harder, but I told her that I am ready because that work for first grade was too easy."

He smiled over at his daughter. "You know, your mom is right. The work will get a little harder, but as long as you try your best, you will be fine. You are one smart cookie."

She smiled up at him and for the second time, he couldn't help the pull at his heart at how long he had been gone.

"None of that son." His mom said taking his attention momentarily away from his little girl. "I see that look in your face, we know why you did what you did and you don't need to beat yourself up about being away."

"Daddy, mommy told me that the Army needed you because you are the best architect there is and she said she knows that if you could do what you do around here that you would not hesitate."

He smiled down at Destiny. "I sure would, but you know since daddy has been away for a while, I think we can make up for that with a little shopping. What do you think?" His daughter's eyes lit up with excitement.

secretive, sneaking around here after hours. I'm not used to her coming in at all hours of the night, that's usually me."

December laughed at her friend. "Has she mentioned a guy's name?"

"Nope she just says she has business to handle but I am not stupid, the only business you handling in the middle of the night is between your legs and some mans."

Leave it to Chaniyah to put it out there. December could always count on Chaniyah to say exactly what was on her mind.

"What's up with you? Where's Destiny?"

"She stayed with her dad."

"Marcel is in town. Girl why didn't you tell me, you know that man is fine. Shoot, if you weren't my girl, I'd jump his bones." Chaniyah started to laugh and December joined in.

"I just found out when I showed up to pick up Destiny and he answered the door. Imagine my surprise."

December went to her kitchen to get a glass of water.

"Well what did he say? Did he mention his divorce?"

"He said that he missed me and wants to take me and Destiny to dinner tomorrow."

Chaniyah started to squeal and December had to pull the phone from her ear.

"Girl that man still wants you. I'm gone have to come over there and work my magic with your make up so you can knock him off his feet."

"No, no, no, no, no." December huffed into the phone. "I am wearing something simple and I am not going to get all dolled up. It's just dinner with our daughter."

Chaniyah sucked her teeth. "Wait, what aren't you telling me? You are holding back, I can feel it. What did he do hug you, kiss you, what?"

December nearly choked on the water she was drinking to chase the two aspirin she had taken to relieve her headache.

"Both." She said really low, almost inaudible.

Chaniyah gasped. "Both. I knew it. Did you kiss him back? Was it earth shattering?"

"One question at a time, sheesh girl. And yes, I kissed him back. It was amazing. It was like there was no time that had went by." December sighed.

"Wait, I'm confused. What's the problem then?"

"The problem is, I don't want to be his rebound. We still don't know why he and Sedora are divorcing. For all we know, he could be still pining after his ex-wife. I just don't want to get my hopes up only to have my heart broken again."

"Sounds to me like he may be the one leaving Sedora. We don't know what the issue is. All you can do is guard your heart and live for the moment. You know we are always here for you regardless. But if he blew your world with a kiss it's obvious there is still a spark there. "

Hours later, December lay in her bed, the conversation that she had with both Chaniyah and Amari still in her head. Maybe she was jumping the gun a little. All Marcel had asked her to do was go to dinner. She had made a fool of herself in front of him for nothing. But when she remembered the kiss they shared, her body heated up. She could still feel his tongue as it glided through her mouth leaving her breathless and panting. The affect he had on her was scary and she was aware of that. She knew she had to guard her heart because if she wasn't careful, she could be right back under his spell. Who was she kidding, she had never been from under his spell. That is why she was still celibate after seven years of being away from him. That was sad.

December looked at the huge pile of clothes on her bed and sighed. When was the last time she got this worked up about going out? She had to remind herself that Destiny was going and that this was just a way for Marcel to have the three of them together. But even as she kept repeating it to herself, she wasn't buying it. She decided finally on a navy-blue shift dress with yellow belt and matching yellow pumps. She opted for a simple ponytail with a couple lose strands in the front. She looked at herself and wondered if perhaps she was overdoing it. Just as she had resolved to change, the doorbell rang. *Just my luck, she thought.* When she opened the door, standing on the other side was Marcel dressed like he came off the cover of GQ and beside him her baby girl in a floral dress with pretty pink shoes and a pink ribbon in her hair.

"Mommy, you look pretty." She smiled down at her baby and kissed her on the cheek.

"Thanks sweetie, you look pretty too." Marcel cleared his throat. December glanced up to see him holding out a floral arrangement.

"These are for you." He said handing them over to December. She took the flowers and as their hands passed through each other, there was a spark that passed through them.

"Thanks Marcel, but you didn't have to get me

flowers." She took the flowers and put them in a vase.

"I know I didn't have to, but I wanted to." He smiled at her. "Are you ready, our reservations are for 7:30?"

"Yes, let me grab my purse."

On the car ride to the restaurant, Destiny talked to December about all of the things that Marcel had bought her the day before. December welcomed the distraction. She hoped that they would arrive to the restaurant soon. She didn't know how much longer she could survive being so close to Marcel. He had on a cologne that was intoxicating. While Destiny continued to talk about her time with her dad, December took the time to let her gaze rake over Marcel. He had on a pair of black slacks and a powder blue button up and a blue and white tie. The way the shirt hugged his muscular frame did things to her insides.

"Like what you see?" Marcel asked when the car stopped at a red light. December feeling embarrassed about being caught staring turned toward the back seat to where her daughter was now resting peacefully. As if following her gaze, "She's been sleep now for about 10 minutes."

"Oh." Was her simple reply.

"You look stunning today December." His heated gaze raked her body from head to foot. "That dress looks like it was made just for you."

"Thank you, you don't look so bad yourself." She gazed at him once more and then before he could catch her staring again, quickly looked out the side window.

"Did I do something wrong last night?" he asked when a moment of silence passed between them.

"No, not at all. Why do you ask?"

"I saw the tears in your eyes D.K. You know I would never intentionally hurt you. I'm trying to understand why you were crying."

"Just let it go Marcel, its complicating."

He didn't say anything for a while and then when he got to another red light he glanced over at her.

"I'm really not that difficult a person to talk to D.K., and I meant what I said yesterday. I really have missed you."

"And what would Sedora think of you missing me?" She spat before she had the chance to police herself. He tightened his grip on the steering wheel.

"She'd probably say that is nothing new, but since we are no longer married, I could care less what she thinks of it. But I do care what you think of it." So, he had finally said it. They were divorced. Surprisingly, it didn't feel as good as it did weeks ago when she had said it to her friends.

"So, what, now that you are divorced I'm the rebound?" Too late to snap her mouth closed now.

"Is that what you think D.K.? Do you think that you could ever be a rebound for me? I thought you knew me better than that."

"I'm sorry Marcel. I'm trying to make since of all of this." The conversation was brought to a halt when they pulled into the restaurant. She started to say something else, but he halted her. "Can we enjoy dinner with our daughter, we can talk later." She nodded. He got out of the car and proceeded to open her door and help her out of the car before lifting his daughter easily out the backseat and resting her head on his shoulders.

"Hamil, reservations for three." He said when they entered the restaurant.

"Right this way Mr. and Mrs. Hamil." The young lady said mistaking them for a married couple. He just smiled and followed her lead.

When she had showed them to their table she

turned and said, "Your waitress name is Bella and she will be with you shortly."

"Thank you." They both replied as the hostess walked off. Marcel woke Destiny up and she took her seat at the table.

The dinner went along smoothly. Marcel and December held light conversation with each other and their daughter. Mainly she and Destiny caught him up on the last two years and he told them about his latest design for a battle craft. Of course, he kept all of the logistics of the craft a secret, but he was very excited about having gotten the contract to design the craft. When the waitress came with the bill at the end of the evening she told them what a lovely family they made. Before December could correct the woman's mistake, Marcel simply replied, "Thank you."

"Mommy that chocolate cake was amazing." Destiny said once they were outside of the restaurant.

"Well you be sure to brush your teeth when we get back to the house okay?"

"Yes ma'am." Then she turned to Marcel and said, "Daddy, are you going to stay at the house with us?"

"Honey, that depends on your mom, I would not

wetness as he massaged her clitoris through the lace material. December nearly came on contact.

Then in one swift motion, Marcel lifted her legs off of the floor and backed her into the bedroom where he laid her on the bed.

"Tell me what you want December. I won't do anything that you don't want me to do." He looked at her with sincerity in his eyes. He was giving her a chance to back out of the situation. In a way, she felt that she should tell him to go in the other room and get in bed and forget they ever kissed, but her body was screaming for her to be reckless and allow a night of passion to ensue. She gazed back at Marcel and then in one smooth move, she removed her night gown and lay before him in nothing but her lace panties.

"I need you to say it baby. Tell me you want me. Your body is telling me you want me, but I need to know that your mind is there too. I don't want regrets tomorrow. If this is not what you want, I will back away. I might have to take a cold shower, but I will be fine. I need to know that we are on the same page. And make no mistake, you could never be a rebound in my book because you have always had my heart. And you always will." She continued to stare at him, passion evident in her eyes.

"Marcel, I need you to make love to me." She

said in a barely audible voice. "I need you inside of me. Please. No regrets." When the words were out of her mouth, he pounced. He removed the remaining of her clothes and proceeded to lavish her body with slow, drugging kisses that sent her plunging over the edge. Marcel re – familiarized himself with her body starting at her neck and working his way down her body. When he reached her midsection, he grasped her hips and then latched onto her for dear life. She cried out at the assault of his tongue. He continued to tease her senses by dragging his tongue in and out, around and over her wetness. She nearly came off of the bed when an orgasm racked her body. Still holding firmly to her hips, Marcel continued to lick until the last shock left her body.

She lay there panting, breathless. He pulled his shirt over his head and removed his under shirt. December watch and reveled at the muscles in his chest. It looked like something off of movies. He could certainly give Boris Kodjoe a run for his money. He lowered his pants to his ankles and casually stepped out of them, never once taking his eyes off of December. Then, like a Lion stalking its prey, he eased up the bed over December and captured her mouth once more in a kiss that was full of so much passion, she almost lost control all over again. He eased his knees between her thighs, prying her legs apart and then in one smooth motion, entered her. The onslaught of his manhood made December's mouth drop open.

"Damn, you're tight baby." He said through gritted teeth. He began with short strokes and then they became long drugging strokes. December thrashed from side to side unable to contain herself as the second orgasm slammed into her.

"That's it baby, come for me." Marcel coached December as an orgasm racked his body. He threw his head back and growled loudly.

December

December awoke the next morning to the smell of bacon and eggs. She stretched and found the spot next to her empty. She looked around and there was no trace of Marcel. In her bathroom she freshened up and then threw on a pair of capris and a tank top. When she walked out of her room she was greeted by her daughter and Marcel.

"Good morning mommy." Destiny said jumping into December's arms.

"Morning sleepy head. We made you breakfast." Marcel said standing at the counter with just his t-shirt and his pants riding low on his hips.

"Morning yourself," was all she managed to say as she took in the sight of him so at home in her kitchen.

"I need to go out to the car and grab some things out of my bag in the trunk. I wanted to wait until you were up." He said coming from behind the counter. He reached where December and Destiny were standing and pressed a light kiss to December's lips.

"Be right back."

When he was out of the apartment, December placed Destiny on her feet and they both walked to the kitchen. Moments later, Marcel came back into the condo and joined them at the table for breakfast. Midway through breakfast, there was a knock at the door.

"I'll get it" Marcel said raising out of his seat and strolling toward the door. Amari and Chaniyah were awe struck when they took in the attire that Marcel had on answering the door.

"Jesus take the wheel," Chaniyah said fanning herself.

Amari shook her head at her friend's tactics and greeted Marcel at the door.

"Hello Marcel, this is a pleasant surprise." She said.

He stepped aside and allowed the two ladies to enter the condo.

"What are y'all doing here?" December asked pleading with her eyes for them not to make a scene.

"What do you mean?" Chaniyah chimed in ignoring her pleading eyes, "Did we come at a bad time? I mean, this is the day we usually come and pick up Destiny for a little fun in the sun. What have you been doing that has jogged your memory?"

December nearly choked on her orange juice and the two friends snickered.

"Well Marcel is in town Chaniyah, I am sure he wants to spend time with Destiny, maybe we can reschedule." Amari said saving December from having to speak.

"It's quite alright ladies, I will be here for a while." He said looking at December. "I don't want to intrude on you all's plans."

Chaniyah looked from December to Marcel. "Well, I'm sure December will keep you busy until we get back." Amari slapped Chaniyah on the back. "What? What did I say?" she asked playfully.

"You know what? Destiny are you ready to go?" Amari asked ignoring Chaniyah.

"Yes, Auntie Mari." She went to December and kissed her and then to Marcel and kissed him.

"See you later mommy and daddy."

"See you sweetheart." They both said.

"You all be good now," Chaniyah said as she exited the condo. December shot her a glare and she closed the door.

"I see Chaniyah is still Chaniyah." Marcel said when silence ensued between him and December.

"Yeah, she isn't going to ever change."

December got up to put her dishes in the sink.

Marcel grabbed the dishes out of her hand, "Here let me do that."

"No, it's the least I can do since you made breakfast. Thanks, by the way." He put his arm around her waist and kissed her deeply. "No problem." He said when he released her. He sat the dishes in the sink and then turned his attention back to December.

"So, tell me something," He said capturing her attention. "When was the last time you were intimate with someone?" December blushed and then tried to recover.

"Why is that any concern of yours?"

"Anything concerning you or my daughter is my concern."

December was taken aback. "You mean anything concerning Destiny is your concern, we are not an item, remember?"

He chuckled and that made her even madder. "Listen Marcel, just because we had sex last night does not mean that you can waltz in here and start inquiring about my sexual life. You don't see me asking you about you and Sedora, so please do not come in here questioning me, okay?" He looked at her for a long moment and then he pulled her into his lap.

"First off, what we did last night was not just sex, we made love. I know you felt it just as well as I did and I refuse to deny what I already know December."

"And what is that Marcel?" she asked trying to pull out of his arms and failing miserably. "Let me go!" she yelled.

"December, stop!" he pleaded. "I love you. I have never stopped loving you and I want to be with you."

"If you loved me, then how could you marry her?" Too late she thought, it was out of her mouth.

Marcel sighed. "December, I was so mad that you could not see that I wanted what was best for you and our baby when I left that I sought love from the first source. Sedora happened to be a willing participant, but I realized early on that I was not in love with her. That is why we got a divorce. I have not touched her in three years. It wasn't fair for me to keep leading her on knowing my heart belongs to you."

"It'll never work Marcel, we have two different

for me? What else will it take?"

"I just need time Marcel. This is happening so fast and I just-"

"I get it. I'm going to go stay at my mom's house. I'm going to give you time to decide what you want. I will not accept part of you December. I need all of you and if you cannot give that to me, then I-I just don't know." He walked out of the room and minutes later December heard the door to the apartment open and close. She lay back on the bed and swipes a frustrated hand down her face.

Where's Daddy?

"Mommy, where's daddy?" Destiny asked the next morning. December patted the bed next to her and Destiny went and joined her mom. "Daddy went to grandma's last night sweetie."

"Is he coming back? I like when daddy stays here. Did I do something wrong?" December saw the pained expression on her daughters' face and blamed herself for it.

"No honey, daddy just wanted to spend some time with grandma that is all. "

"Will he stay tonight here mommy?"

"I don't know sweetheart but just know that daddy loves you very much and even if he decides not to stay here, it does not change how he feels about you." She hugged Destiny. "Shall we eat some breakfast before I take you to grandmas?"

"Yes mommy."

After breakfast, December dressed both herself and Destiny. She packed her lunch for work and then dropped Destiny off over Marcel's mother's house. Her ride to work was eerily silent and she said.

"You sure it's not you that likes the place." Amari says playfully. Chaniyah flashes her a playful hurt look.

"You two are a piece of work." Marcel said. "But I really appreciate all that you guys have done in the past couple days. Truly, from the bottom of my heart, I thank you guys."

"You gone make me cry. We would do anything for December. She is as close to a blood sister that I have ever had." Amari said fighting tears.

"Oh Lord, let me get her sensitive ass out of here before she starts with the water works." Chaniyah says grabbing Destiny's overnight bag and leading Amari towards the door. "Come on, I want to try out that dance revolution game." They walked out of the condo laughing, leaving December with her thoughts and Marcel, of course.

After a moment of silence, Marcel says to December, "So we're going to have another baby huh?"

"It seems so," December said dropping her head so he wouldn't see the tears welling up in her eyes.

"D.K., look at me." Marcel said pulling

December's chin up so that they were at eye level. "I extended my leave for another month. I meant what I said December, I want to be here for you and Destiny. I will do whatever it takes to make us a family and now that we are about to have another baby, I want more than anything for us to officially be a family."

"You make it sound like it is so simple Marcel." She sighed. "You have your life in the Army, and Destiny and I have our lives here. I don't expect you to drop what you are doing and be here with Destiny and I and I hope you wouldn't ask that of me."

"D.K., I may not have all of the answers right now, but you have to believe that we can make this work if we are both willing to put in effort. We could counsel with Chaniyah, whatever we need to do, tell me baby and we will do it, but I will not walk away again without having my family intact."

"Marcel..."

"No December, stop fighting it. Admit it, we are good together. What are you so afraid of? I love you and I love Destiny. And the baby you are carrying, I love it too! The fact that it was conceived in our love making, I feel an attachment to it already. "

The dam inside of December broke and she began

"December you made a beautiful bride," her friends were saying as they sat around at the reception.

"Thanks guys and it means so much to me that you guys were able to get dresses at such a late notice. I really appreciate you guys."

"Anything for our sistah friend. "

Just then, Amari excused herself from the table in a hurry. The friends looked at each other with confusion etched in their features.

"What's up with her?" December asked.

"Beats the hell out of me. " Chaniyah said. "She's been acting really weird lately. I think her and Cameron are not seeing each other anymore. She hasn't been out lately."

"Well has she said anything?" December asked.

"Nope, she locks herself in her room, but I be hearing her sniffling on the other end. Something is definitely wrong."

Just then, Amari returns to the table, her face looked flush and appeared to be dry like she had recently wiped it with a dry napkin or towel.

"Okay, what gives Amari and please don't give us the watered down, nothing to report just hanging with a friend bull crap you have been feeding, we want the truth." Chaniyah said and December and Fentress both shook their heads in agreement.

"Well I haven't heard from Cameron for the past two weeks. He was calling me regularly and we were seeing each other and we spent a few nights together at his place and then poof, nothing. Every time I call his phone, it's going straight to his voicemail. I'm so confused. I was ready to tell you guys that things were going well and thinking I had finally found someone who really made me happy and then this." She dabbed at a tear that was threatening to escape her eyes.

"Aww honey, I'm sorry to hear that. Maybe something happened. Have you been by his place?"

"Yes and I have not seen his car there or anything. It just doesn't make sense."

Chaniyah, ever the observant one looks at Amari and sees something familiar in her features. "What aren't you telling us?"

"I'm   pregnant!"   She   blurted   out.

passion in the bedroom. She shook the thought out of her head, as it was very unprofessional. Her cheeks heated as she chastised herself for the way her mind was going.

"Well Cameron, I have to say that we do have a pretty decent case load these days. I don't know that any of my accountants have the extra time to take on another client. "

"Well it's like this Amari, I'm glad that they don't since I want you to personally handle it."

Taken aback momentarily she responded, "Cameron, no disrespect but my time is highly valuable and I like to keep my case load modest so that I can keep an eye on the running of the other clients that are in our employ."

"Which is why I am willing to pay top dollar to see to it that you are the one who is in charge of my company. Pleasure is like my baby, and I don't want just anyone handling it. I choose you because I admire your dedication to your company and what you have been able to achieve over the years is commendable. This is not my first nightclub; however, this is the first one that I have built from the ground so to me, this one means the most to me." She pondered over his request momentarily. She knew what it was like to start a company from the ground and build it up. She was no stranger to hard work, but here lately, she had scaled back to being the one to look over the paperwork making sure that her accountants were accurate, because her company was known for its accuracy. His request would mean that she would be taking work home again and she wasn't sure she was ready to go back to that.

"How about you come out to the club this evening and I can give you a tour, show you what we are about and then, you can get back to me with an answer. I really want you on this account." He handed her a file. "I have prepared this just to give you the logistics of the day to day operations and what the request would require of you." She took the file and their hands touched in the exchange causing her body to respond. She had to wonder if she was so hesitant because of the way her body was responding to him. She would usually welcome any business to her company because it meant another source of revenue.

She glanced over the file. "These reports are impeccable, why would you want to outsource your AR and AP?"

"Well Amari, I need to be able to be on the forefronts to run the managing of the club and I can better accomplish that if I do not have to do the work myself. It is my goal to keep my nightclub as upscale as possible and I need to be able to keep an eye on the day to day and I cannot do that when I am buried in paperwork behind the confines of my office." She stared at him for a moment and then back to the documents in front of her. It did seem like quite a bit of work and she could see how that would stop him from accomplishing his goal for the club. However, that was the very reason she was questioning whether she wanted to take on the case load to begin with.

"Please Amari, come out to the club tonight and let me show you around?"

"I'm not a big socializer, but how about I stop by as you are closing up. Here's my card, give me a call, once you are close to closing and I will do my best to come out."

"Okay, it's a week night so we usually close around ten, will that work for you?" She thought about it.

"That'll be find Cameron." She said coming from behind her desk to walk him out. "It was a pleasure to meet you and thanks again for considering my company for your business needs."

He accepted her outstretched hand. "The pleasure was all mines Amari, I look forward to seeing you later." And with that he was out of her office.

The rest of the workday was uneventful as she reviewed client records making sure that her accountants were reporting and accurately documenting for the clients she had worked so hard to get. She found herself thinking about Cameron a few times while she was at the office. It had been so long since she had been remotely interested in anyone. She simply did not want to get involved simply for the sake of being involved. Too many women felt they needed a man to validate them and then, most men were threatened by women who had good paying jobs and if they weren't threatened, they were looking for a free ride. She wondered how Cameron felt about women who could hold their own and then wondered why it mattered. She hated to admit it to herself, but she liked him.

About the Author

Angel Bunton-Miller has been writing since the age of 15 years old. She started out writing poetry and had several published in anthologies in the 6th grade. Her first two books she had published, she wrote at the age of 15. Recently divorced, Angel is a mother of three. She has a Bachelor's of Science in Business Accounting. When she isn't writing, Angel loves to sew. She is currently working on starting her own clothing line. Look for book two "Conceived in Love" very soon.

Made in the USA
Middletown, DE
24 September 2021